Cassandra's Driftwood

Cassandra's Driftwood

Budge Wilson

illustrated by Terry Roscoe

Pottersfield Press, Lawrencetown Beach,
Nova Scotia, Canada
1994

Canadian Cataloguing in Publication

Wilson, Budge -

Cassandra's Driftwood

ISBN 0-919002-85-8

I. Roscoe, Terry. II. Title.

PS8595.I5813C37 1994   jC813'.54   C94-950055-0

PZ7.W45Ca 1994

Reprinted 2003

Pottersfield Press gratefully acknowledges the ongoing support of the Nova Scotia Department of Tourism and Culture and the Canada Council.

Pottersfield Press
Lawrencetown Beach
R.R. 2, Porters Lake
Nova Scotia B0J 2S0

Printed in Canada

This book is for

my grandson

Nicholas Jarche

with love

Chapter One: Cassandra

Cassandra Westhaver lived in a small fishing village beside the sea. In the village there were fifteen fish-houses, thirteen wharves, thirty-six boats and nineteen regular houses. Her father owned one of the fish-houses, one of the wharves, three of the boats and a regular house.

It was a beautiful place to live. The sun rose in the morning over the sea and set in the evening behind the wooded hill to the west. The fish-houses were painted many bright and happy colours.

But Cassandra couldn't always enjoy the sun and the sea and the thirty-six boats. Sometimes she had too much on her mind to notice them. Even when she was looking right at them, it was as though they weren't there. She was too busy looking at what was going on inside her own head.

There are two important things that you need to know about Cassandra. The first thing is this:

She was very shy.

The second is this:

She owned a piece of driftwood which she loved.

Now let me tell you more about both of those things.

Chapter Two: Inside the Box

Cassandra hated being shy. She watched other children as they played, as they talked to their friends, as they argued with their parents, and as they got to know each other. She wished she could be just like those kids. Everything they did looked so easy.

But not for Cassandra. Things weren't easy at all.

There was a whole lot of stuff piled up inside her that wanted to come out. Here is what some of it was:

- She wanted to ask Suzanne Davidson to stop calling her Cassie.

- She wanted to tell her mother that she hated piano lessons and that she'd love to take dancing instead. If you have to drive for fifty-five minutes once a week to take a lesson, you might as well be learning something you like.

- Cassandra also wanted to tell her teacher that she couldn't see the chalkboard from the back of the room.

- And another thing. A new girl had moved into the yellow house that was down beside the beach. Her name was Lindy. She had wild red curls and a big wide grin. When she thought something was funny, you could hear her laugh clear across the schoolyard. Cassandra wanted to march right up to Lindy and say, "I'd like you to be my best friend."

Cassandra often did all of those things in her head. Sometimes when she was alone in the house, she even practised saying them out loud.

But when Cassandra took a deep breath and tried to say them to Suzanne or her mother or her teacher or Lindy, she couldn't get her tongue to work. It just wouldn't move. It stuck to the roof of her mouth while her teeth stayed clamped tight shut. She felt as though she were trapped in a box with her shyness sitting on the lid. She wanted like anything to get out.

Chapter Three: A Great Catch

Now I'll tell you about Cassandra's driftwood.

One day, when Cassandra was sitting on her father's wharf, minding her own business, her piece of driftwood came to her - moving along on the incoming tide, heading straight for the ladder. The driftwood was huge. It was way bigger than she was. It had a lot of branches and roots and spiky places. Right away, Cassandra knew that she had to have it.

She climbed down the ladder to the surface of the water and caught the driftwood as it floated in towards shore. She had a rope all ready, tied to the top rung of the ladder. She twisted the free end around two of the driftwood's spikes and then ran to find her father.

When Cassandra found her father, he was unloading mackerel from his seine boat at the Government Wharf. That morning he'd dragged in two seine boats behind his motorboat, and they were full of fish. He was very busy. But Cassandra's face looked so full of desperation that he left his fish and followed her.

"Hurry!" she said.

"What's wrong?" he asked.

"Nothing's wrong," she said. "Everything's right. A wonderful thing just came in on the tide, but it might get away if we don't pull it up on land."

"Well then," he said, "why didn't you do that?"

"Too big," she panted as they rushed along the shore to the Westhaver's wharf.

When Mr. Westhaver saw the driftwood, he laughed.

"That's just a big hunk of wood," he said. "Do you really want *that*?"

"Yes," she said. "I want it a lot. I love it." For a moment, she was not one bit shy.

Something had opened up the lid of the box she was trapped in and a piece of her squeezed out.

"*Weird*," muttered her father. "Sometimes I think I'll never understand women."

But Mr. Westhaver could see the look in Cassandra's eyes. He couldn't say no to *that*.

The tide was still pretty low and he was wearing his hip waders. He walked into the water and tightened the rope on the wood. Then he dragged it in to shore and looked at it.

Just a dumb piece of wood, he thought.

He was all ready to kick it out to sea again, but he was stopped by the wild joy on Cassandra's face.

Mr. Westhaver picked up one end of the wood and Cassandra picked up the other end. They carried it to a flat place on the edge of the cliff, not far from the Westhaver's house, close to the path that led to the beach. Then they put it down. It settled firmly onto the grass, as steady as could be - just as though it were growing right out of the ground.

"It's where it belongs," said Cassandra, sighing and hugging herself. "Thank you."

Mr. Westhaver returned to his mackerel, shaking his head as he walked along.

Chapter Four: Alonzo

Cassandra sat down on the grass and looked at the piece of driftwood.

It looked like a person - a strange but wonderful person, all full of angles and bumps and spikes. The legs were the roots, and they were twisted into a graceful sitting position on the ground.

The arms were branches, and they seemed to be doing many different things. What they did depended on which way you looked at them.

The spikes were where branches had broken off, and they were the ears and the chin and the nose. Cassandra picked up two pebbles and pushed them into two small holes. "Eyes," she said. Then she sat close beside the piece of driftwood, and tried to put herself into all the different positions that the tree was in. "He's a dancer," Cassandra decided. "I'll call him Alonzo." She couldn't remember where the name Alonzo came from. Maybe out of a book.

Cassandra went back to the house and got a little chair out of the attic. She put it down on the grass close to Alonzo. As the days went by, she would often sit on the chair beside him, reading a book or writing in her diary or looking at the view. Sometimes she would feed the seagulls scraps of fish, and they would come and sit on Alonzo's head and on his arms. She felt very contented there, close to Alonzo.

Cassandra could imagine that Alonzo was many things besides a dancer. Sometimes she'd put a sou'wester on his head and a net in his hand. Then he'd be a fisherman.

Another time she'd put a gull feather on his head and a pipe in his hand, and then Alonzo would be a Micmac chief, smoking

his peace pipe and spreading peacefulness all around him.

She dressed him up in many ways, and he became a priest, a soldier, an actor, a magician.

"Better than a doll," said Cassandra. "Or a teddy bear. Or maybe even a best friend." But she wasn't so sure about that. Cassandra had some friends, but no *best* friend. She was too shy to ask important questions or to tell special secrets - and those are two of the things that best friends do. She thought she'd like to do those things with Lindy.

Never mind. She had Alonzo. She talked to him. And she listened to what he said.

Sometimes her mother would say, "Why don't you go off and play with your friends? Why stay around here all by yourself so much of the time?"

"I'm not alone," Cassandra would say. "I'm with Alonzo. I talk to him, and he takes the lid off my box."

Mrs. Westhaver sighed. She had no idea what Cassandra was talking about. "O.K.," she said as she went back to her work. "Do whatever makes you happy."

Chapter Five: Gone!

One day in May, Mr. and Mrs. Westhaver went to Halifax to do some business. They asked a sitter to come and mind the dog and the cat, and to be there when Cassandra came home from school. Her name was Mrs. Hotchkiss.

At four o'clock, Cassandra climbed down from the school bus and started up the path to her house. Her head was bent down as she walked along. That day, she had *almost* worked up enough courage to ask Lindy to be her best friend. But she hadn't quite managed it. The lid on her box was shut down too tight. Cassandra was so mad at that box that all she could do was

stomp along and stare at the ground. Sometimes she kicked a stone.

It was a beautiful day - warm and sunny
- but Cassandra felt too sad to enjoy it. The
gulls were squawking and calling out their
many harsh songs, but she didn't even
hear them. Her misery shut her ears up
tight. So, as soon as she'd helped herself to
a cookie and said hi to Mrs. Hotchkiss, she
went out to sit with Alonzo.

He wasn't there.

There was just a little scuffed-up place
on the grass where he used to be.

Cassandra couldn't even think. She had
a terrible fear inside herself, and it drove
her across the field like a wild deer. She
pushed open the back door and stood in
the middle of the kitchen.

"Mrs. Hotchkiss!" she shrieked. Mrs.
Hotchkiss came racing down the stairs to
see what was the matter.

"He's *gone!*" Cassandra yelled. "Where
did he *go?*"

"Who?" asked Mrs. Hotchkiss, holding
Cassandra by the shoulders to calm her
down. "What on earth are you talking
about?"

"Alonzo!" screamed Cassandra, shaking herself loose from Mrs. Hotchkiss's hands. "He's gone!"

Mrs. Hotchkiss had never seen Cassandra so frantic and noisy. She didn't know that Cassandra had just jumped right out of her box.

After a lot of questions and a lot of yelling from Cassandra, Mrs. Hotchkiss finally asked,"Who in the name of time is Alonzo?"

"My driftwood," wailed Cassandra, who could hardly speak now. Her words were coming out of her in chunks, instead of in sentences. "Huge. Out on the cliff. Lots of branches and roots. Silver grey. Beautiful. My friend. Gone!"

"O dear, O dear, O dear, O dear!" cried Mrs. Hotchkiss, her fist flying to her mouth. "I gave it away."

Cassandra was howling again. "Gave him *away*?" she yelled.

"Yes," sighed Mrs. Hotchkiss. "A bunch of teenagers came by and said they were having a big bonfire and sing-song on the beach tonight. They said the driftwood would be perfect for the centre of the fire. They said the flames would shoot straight up the trunk into the air. So I gave it to them. I thought it was just a big hunk of wood."

Cassandra wasn't screaming anymore. In a very low and terrible voice, full of grief, she said, "*Just a big hunk of wood!*"

Then Cassandra stood up very straight. The fear she was feeling now was bigger than any fear she'd ever had about the lid coming off her box. "Which beach?" she demanded. "Which way did they go?"

By now, the sun was low in the sky and it would be dark before too long. It would be a good time to light a bonfire.

"White Sands Beach," said Mrs. Hotchkiss. "They went by way of the beach path. About an hour ago. I'm really sorry, Cassandra. I didn't realize." Then she went into the kitchen to get supper ready.

An hour ago! Cassandra felt her wildness coming back. Anything could happen in an hour.

Chapter Six: Path of Fear

Without another word, Cassandra flew out the back door and raced over the field to the shore path that led to the beach. Mrs. Hotchkiss didn't even see her go.

It was getting darker now, and part of the sky had clouded over. Cassandra stopped for a moment and looked ahead.

All around her there were things that she usually found frightening. The shore path was uneven, and the dark woods came right down to the edge of the cliff. Rustlings in the bushes told her that there were animals in there - porcupines, raccoons...*bears*? Ahead was the long, long path to the beach, and after that, the lovely broad expanse of sand leading down to the sea.

Cassandra loved the beach, with its rolling waves pounding on the shore. But this time it would be a scary place. There would be a bunch of teenagers down there and maybe a huge and terrible fire.

Cassandra was shy with kids her own age, but with teenagers she was almost paralyzed. They were so big and bossy and noisy and *sure*. They thought they were kings and queens of every castle. They thought that kids like her were for pushing around and scolding and yelling at.

Cassandra came very close to turning around and slinking home. Then she thought again about Alonzo and the pillar of flames that might be shooting out of his head at that very moment.

She clenched her fists hard and ran through the bushes onto the shore path. She raced over the uneven ground, hardly even hearing the noises in the woods - squeaks and shuffles and crackling branches. She paid no attention to the gathering darkness. She didn't even think about what she'd do when she found all

those older kids. Her one biggest fear shoved every other fear right out of her head.

It was a long path, but suddenly she was there. In the woods it had been almost completely dark, but here on the beach there was still the light from a blazing sunset. For a moment, Cassandra thought that the red light in the sky was from the bonfire, but it wasn't. Far down the beach, she could see a group of the teenagers - maybe fifteen of them - crowded around a giant pile of wood. And on top of that whole mountain of firewood was Alonzo, his arms raised to the sky.

Chapter Seven: A Fierce Kid

Most people would have been too tired
to move after that long run through the
woods. But not Cassandra. With her eyes
fixed on Alonzo, she raced across the firm
sand, feeling like a cheetah on the hunt -
the swiftest animal in the world. But she
didn't think about that for very long. Her
mind was so full of Alonzo that there was
no room for anything else.

As Cassandra got closer and closer to
the big kids, she could see them trying to
light matches in the strong night wind.
Faster and faster she ran, but she still had
enough energy to yell.

"Stop! Stop! Stop!" she screamed, waving her arms around. "*Stop!*"

Finally the teenagers heard her, and they dropped their matches in the sand, watching as she came shrieking across the beach.

"The kid's crazy," one of them said.

"Man! What a racket!" said another.

"Must be out of her tree," said a third.

A fourth one looked at her - very cool, with his hands in his pockets - as she reached the group. "Stop *what*?" he drawled.

But he couldn't keep her from screaming. Now she was yelling, "He's *mine*! He's *mine*!"

"*Who's* yours?" asked the same boy, leaning down until his face was almost touching hers. "Quit hollering," he growled. "Try talking."

"Alonzo," she said, panting to catch her breath. "The big piece of driftwood on top of the pile. He's mine. I own him. You took him from my cliff. I came to get him."

"Ha!" snorted a girl in tight leather pants with hot pink hair. "Yours in the morning, maybe. *Ours, tonight.* Get lost, kid."

Cassandra had stopped being shy the minute she had seen that Alonzo was missing. But she still wasn't sure how she could get him off that mountain of wood and away from those tough kids. Then, all of a sudden she knew.

With a speed that even a cheetah would envy, Cassandra climbed up the woodpile - a pile that was as high as the top of the Westhaver's woodshed - and stood on top. Now she and Alonzo were alone on the roof of the world. She put her arm around his waist and spoke softly to him. "Don't worry," she said. "They can't burn you up without burning me up, too. And they won't do that." Then she added, "I hope."

At last she spoke to the teenagers. "Your hotdogs are getting sandy in the wind," she called down. "And little sand flies are crawling all over them. Aren't you hungry? Let me and Alonzo come down, and then you can light your fire."

A big boy tried to climb up the woodpile to get Cassandra, but he was too

heavy and the pieces of wood kept break-
ing when he stepped on them.

A girl tried to scramble up, but she
began slipping around and turning her
ankle. So she finally gave up.

Someone tried to make the woodpile col-
lapse by pulling sticks out of the bottom.
But the pile was too heavy. All it did was
jiggle a little.

At last, one boy, who seemed to be their
leader, said, "I'm hungry. We don't need
her stupid piece of wood. Besides, we
might get in trouble. This kid seems to be
pretty fierce. She must know something we
don't know. Maybe her father's a
policeman or a Fisheries Inspector or something." Then he yelled up to Cassandra,
"O.K., kid. C'mon down. You can have
your dumb hunk of wood. We never really
liked it in the first place."

So Cassandra gave Alonzo the gentlest
of shoves, and slowly, slowly, he slid over
the pile onto the ground. As she climbed
down, she repeated to herself, *This kid
seems to be pretty fierce.* Cassandra felt as
though she were tall enough to touch the
star that had just come out above her head.

Two of the big kids took Alonzo and carried him halfway to the shore path. Then one of them said, "That's it, kid. Now *you* can figure out how to get it back home."

Chapter Eight: Lindy

Cassandra stood on the beach and watched as the huge pile of wood burst into flames. Higher and higher grew the fire, and sparks flew into the air, raining down on the sand. She could see the teenagers moving around the bonfire with long sticks, roasting their hotdogs in the glowing coals. Against the vivid red light, beside the pounding surf, they looked like dancing witches.

Cassandra hugged Alonzo. "It's alright," she whispered. "I'm a pretty fierce kid. I'll look after you." Then she heard a sound behind her.

It was Lindy. Just standing there, smiling. Cassandra had forgotten that her house was right beside the beach.

Cassandra looked at Lindy for only a very brief moment before she spoke.

"Hi, Lindy," she said. "Would you like to be my best friend?"

"Yes," grinned Lindy. "I sure would!" Then she said, "My mother wants to know if you need some help."

"Yes, please," said Cassandra. "I need someone to help me carry Alonzo to a safe place. Maybe to your house. Till tomorrow morning. Then my father will come and get him."

Lindy didn't say, "Why do you want that stupid piece of wood?" Instead, she went to get her father, and together the three of them carried Alonzo to the fenced-off pen behind the woodshed.

"Looks like a person," said Lindy. "A dancer, maybe. I hope he won't mind spending the night with the chickens."

"He'll love it," said Cassandra.

Chapter Nine: Out of the Box

Suddenly Cassandra could hear someone calling her name, and out from the
shore path ran Mrs. Hotchkiss, waving a
flashlight. "Cassandra!" she gasped. "You
scared me half to death! Rushing off when
my back was turned! What on earth did
you do a thing like that for?"

"Because I had to," explained Cassandra.
And a good thing, too, she thought. She
sniffed the air. She wanted to discover
what the air felt like outside the box. It felt
good.

On the way home, Mrs. Hotchkiss was
too tired and out of breath to talk. Cas-

sandra was glad of that, because she had a lot of thinking to do. And plans to make.

She could hardly wait to tell Lindy a whole lot of important secrets. And she had all kinds of questions she wanted to ask. Like:

What was Lindy's favourite colour?

Did she have a cat? A dog, maybe?

Did her older sister tease her?

Did she like adding and subtracting?

What kind of dreams did she have at night?

Did she have day-dreams in the daytime?

What TV programme did she like best?

What would she choose for a treat? Ice-cream or popcorn? Or both?

Important things like that.

Just before Cassandra dropped off to sleep that night, she had other thoughts.

Tomorrow she'd tell her teacher that she couldn't see the chalkboard. Then she'd probably get glasses, and be able to make out the pattern on her mother's kerchief. And perhaps even pine needles and blades of grass that were far away.

She was sure that Suzanne would stop calling her Cassie if she asked her. On the other hand, maybe Cassie was an O.K. name. Maybe it meant that Suzanne liked her. "Cassie. Cassie." Cassandra said it out loud. Not half bad. In her head, she could hear herself saying to Lindy, "You can call me Cassandra if you want. But my friends call me Cassie." She smiled.

Just then the door of her bedroom opened, and her mother came in to check if she was covered. Back from Halifax, thought Cassandra. She was very sleepy, but she reached up her arms to hug her mother.

"I'd much rather take dancing lessons," she said.

Then she fell asleep.

Other Books by Budge Wilson

The Best Worst Christmas Present Ever
Mr. John Bertrand Nijinsky and Charlie
A House Far From Home
Mystery Lights at Blue Harbour
Breakdown
Thirteen Never Changes
Going Bananas
Madame Belzile & Ramsay Hitherton-Hobbs
The Leaving
Lorinda's Diary
Oliver's Wars
The Courtship

In 1993, Budge Wilson won the Ann Connor Brimer Award for children's literature for **Oliver's Wars**. Her books have been picked for the "Our Choice" selections from the Canadian Children's Books Centre. She has also won the CBC Literary Competition, The Dartmouth Book Award and the Canadian Library Association YA Book Award.

Budge was born in Halifax and was educated at Dalhousie University and the University of Toronto. She went on to be a columnist on child care for the **Globe and Mail**, a book illustrator and a fitness instructor. After 33 years in Ontario, Budge moved back to Nova Scotia to live by the sea on the South Shore.

Illustrator Terry Roscoe was born in Nova Scotia, graduated from Acadia University and works as a bookkeeper in Annapolis Royal. She lives in the woods near Annapolis with her husband, three daughters, three cats and a dog. She has also illustrated Budge Wilson's novel, **Mr. John Nijinsky and Charlie**.